Magemother

· A Novella ·

The Empty Throne

Austin J. Bailey

Copyright © 2015 by Austin J. Bailey.

All rights reserved. No part of this publication may be reproduced, distributed or transmitted in any form or by any means, including photocopying, recording, or other electronic or mechanical methods, without the prior written permission of the publisher, except in the case of brief quotations embodied in critical reviews and certain other noncommercial uses permitted by copyright law. For permission requests, write to the publisher at the address below. Please contact by email.

Austin Bailey

www.austinjbailey.com

Email address: austin@austinjbailey.com

Note: This is a work of fiction. All characters, places, and incidents are a product of the author's imagination. Any resemblance to actual people, living or dead, or to businesses, companies, events, institutions, or locales is entirely coincidental.

Cover design by James T. Egan, www.bookflydesign.com.

Edited by Crystal Watanabe, www.pikkoshouse.com.

Map of Aberdeen by Karl Vesterberg, www.traditionalmaps.com.

Printed in the United States of America

Author's Note:

The problem with sidekicks is that they are often overshadowed by the main character. They don't get a chance to talk about where they came from, what they are worried about, or how they ended up in the story. In Tabitha's case, this just didn't seem right. She's too good, too wonderful a person, in my opinion, not to get her very own story.

This is it.

Contents

Part One
In which there are three queens - 1

Part Two
In which there is a dragon - 8

Part Three
In which there is an empty throne - 23

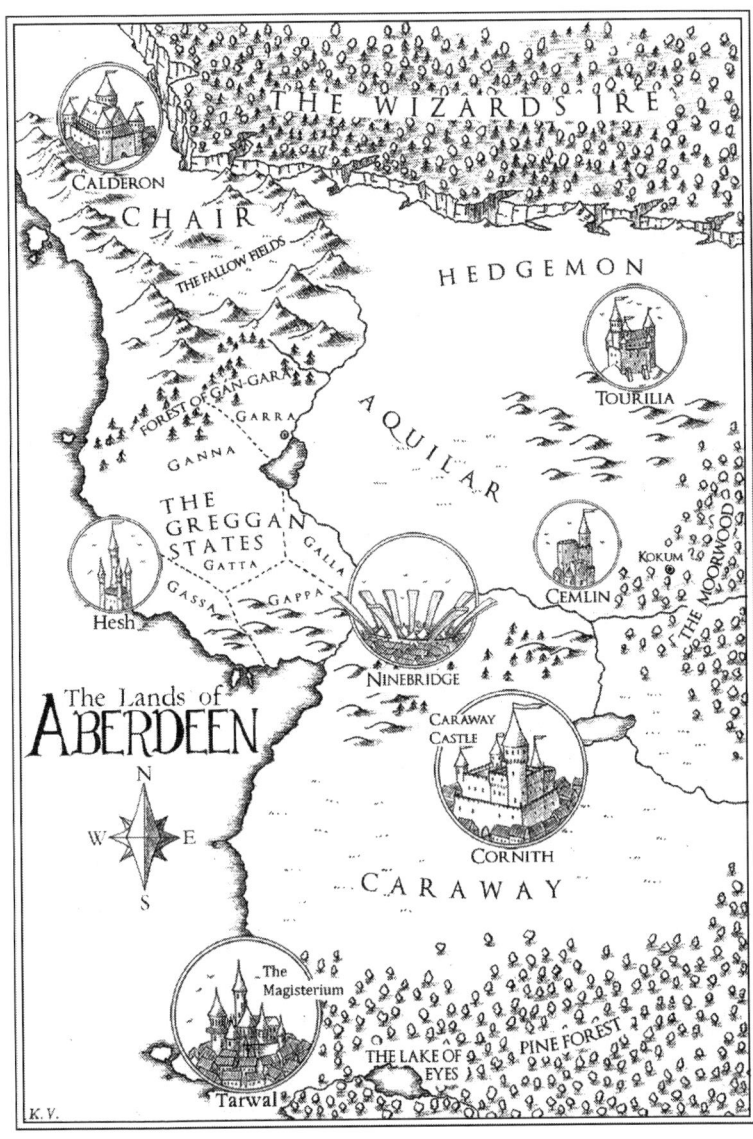

Part One

In which there are three queens

TABITHA FOLLOWED THE MAN with the hat down a long stone walkway that led from the king's castle and out onto the city streets. She took the form of a cat at first, black as night, padding along quietly behind him, then an owl, silent and swift. Then she became a gnat that landed atop his black bowler hat and sat there, bobbing up and down in the lamplight, wondering what in the world Archibald was doing in the middle of the night all dressed up when he should be sleeping.

The hat weaved through the maze of streets, through the gates, out of the city, and through a beautiful moonlit meadow. By that time, Tabitha's reservations about spying on the king's most trusted advisor had vanished. Not because she thought he was being deceitful; that had never crossed her mind. Archibald was one of the best people in the world, and he was the Magemother's friend, the old Magemother as well as the new Magemother, which was good enough for Tabitha. She was glad she came because of the beauty of the night. The sky was clear, revealing a wealth of silver and gold light that mirrored the beauty of the meadow below. Nightbells bloomed in the tall grass around them, flashing blue and purple in the moonlight, and the scent of wild rosemary met her with every slight gust of wind.

At the end of the meadow, they came to the lake, and Archibald took off his hat and his starched white gloves and laid aside his cane. He sat down on the smooth stones by the lake's edge with his hat in his lap, the small gnat on the brim going unnoticed. He removed a white rose bud from the breast pocket of his jacket and began picking off the petals. One by one, he breathed on them and threw them onto the still surface of the lake, adding white satin flecks to a field of reflected stars. Finally, he whispered, "Halis."

At first, nothing happened. Then, quite suddenly, like the very first drop of rain, a face appeared in the water, just beneath the surface, staring up at him expectantly. It was a woman's face. She broke the surface of the water, dashing the stars apart. "Archibald," she said reproachfully, rising halfway out of the water. "You are not the Magemother."

"I am her husband."

"Still, you should not summon me so."

Archibald tore his eyes away from her and studied his feet. "I know."

She brushed an ivory web of hair from her face; it fell across skin the color of sunlit sapphire. Her voice was a sleepy river, gentle, deep. "Still, I am not displeased. I have no one to speak to these days, apart from my sisters."

Archibald looked up hopefully. "I have few people to speak to also."

She smiled. "So... it will be just you and I tonight, like the old days, the king's confidant and the Queen of the Water Nymphs, sharing secrets with each other that should not cross the water."

Archibald nodded wearily. "I would like that. I need someone to tell me if I am a fool."

She grinned slyly. "No doubt you are. But Archibald, what would your friend ask of me? Or were you not aware that you brought someone with you tonight?"

Archibald frowned. The water nymph flicked her finger like she would flick a gnat, and the gnat on Archibald's hat tumbled through the air, turning into Tabitha.

"Tabitha!" Archibald exclaimed, jumping to his feet. He looked more shocked than angry, for which Tabitha was grateful; she had not planned on being caught. "Hi, Archibald," was the best thing she could think of to say. Then, "Your friend is very beautiful." As an afterthought, she added, "Sorry," because she knew he probably hadn't wanted to be followed.

"Tabitha," Archibald said, taking control of himself, "you should not follow me like that. Did the Magemother ask you to spy on me?"

"No, I was just curious where you were going."

Archibald nodded, looking relieved.

"Please don't send me away, Archibald," Tabitha said.

"Very well," he said, sighing. "But if you stay, you must promise not to speak of what you hear."

"Oh," she said. "I promise." She turned to Halis, excitement in her voice. "I've never met a nymph before. Is that what you are?"

"Yes," the nymph said, gliding closer.

"Are there many water nymphs in Aberdeen?" Tabitha asked curiously.

"There are many," Halis said, inching closer still. "But not in Aberdeen. There are also three nymph queens." She glanced stiffly at Archibald. "Though there used to be four."

"Used to be? What happened? Did she die? Oh, don't say she died." Tabitha laid down on the bank beside Archibald and folded her hands under her chin with the attitude of one settling down for a good story. Archibald gave a resigned sigh.

"She didn't die," the nymph said, smiling sweetly. She moved closer, so close that Tabitha could almost reach out and touch her hair, if she wished. "She was taken from the nymph kingdom by the gods. They made her into the Magemother. Then Archibald here," she said, slapping the water and splashing him, "married her."

Tabitha gasped, staring at Archibald with wide eyes. "Really? So that's where she came from! I had no idea. Nobody ever talks about who she was before she was the Magemother." Tabitha paused, thinking. "Nymphs aren't listed among the creatures that Belterras is teaching me about," Tabitha said, looking curiously at Halis. "I don't know anything about you."

"Belterras," the nymph said, looking at Archibald. He nodded, confirming something to her. "You are his apprentice?" she asked.

Tabitha nodded several times. "He says I will be the Mage of Earth one day, like he is now." She sighed. "There is so much to learn, though. I have to learn the shapes of all the animals, their voices, their thoughts. He says I have to know them as well as my own. They will all be under my care someday...even you, I suppose..."

Halis laughed. "Silly child," she said. "I am not an animal to be cared for by some petty mage. I am a nymph!"

Tabitha gaped at her, horrified at her mistake. "Oh," she said. "I'm terribly sorry. I didn't mean any offense."

Halis eyed Tabitha skeptically. "Perhaps," she said.

Tabitha cleared her throat, deciding to change the subject. "How do you know Belterras, then?" she asked.

Halis pursed her lips. "Well," she said slowly, "though we do not depend on him for survival, the Mage of Earth was responsible for the creation of our kingdom."

"Really?" Tabitha said. Belterras had not mentioned it to her in their lessons.

"Yes," Halis said. "Long ago the nymph people dwelt on the land, sharing it with your people, but..." She wrinkled her nose. "We did not get along. Rather than risk outright war between our people, the Mages of Earth and Sea placed us in our own kingdom. Belterras maintains the magic that keeps our world safely out of yours."

Tabitha nodded. "So someday, I will maintain it for you," she said.

The nymph squinted at her. "Perhaps," she said again softly.

Tabitha sighed. "Well, you're very beautiful, anyway. Are your sisters as pretty as you are? Where are they?" She looked around, as if they might appear at any minute.

"You should hope they do not come," Halis murmured. "They are very curious about mortals. Even more curious than I." Without warning, her blue arm shot from the water like a snake, reaching for Tabitha. Archibald, who had been expecting something of the sort, grabbed Tabitha by the hem of her cloak and jerked her back to safety.

Halis smacked the water with the flat of her hand, pouting. "Come now, Archibald. You spoil my fun."

"My sincerest apologies," he said, patting Tabitha on the back.

"I haven't seen the Mage of Earth for an age," Halis protested. "I miss talking with him. He used to show me the most wonderful creatures," she said. She looked up, contemplating something only she could see, and a smile touched her lips. "Things you cannot ever see from the water." She scowled suddenly at Archibald. "I quite think stealing his apprentice would have won me a visit from him."

"I can show you animals," Tabitha said enthusiastically. She danced out of Archibald's grasp, flitting from the rocks into the air, changing into a large monarch butterfly with wings the color of sunshine. She fluttered out over the water.

The nymph reached for her, fingers clutching at delicate wings, but the butterfly danced skillfully away to the shore again, changing back into Tabitha.

"Yes! Beautiful!" Halis was clapping her hands gleefully. "Again! Again!"

Tabitha smiled and changed into a deer.

"I see all kinds of deer." Halis yawned, unimpressed. She scowled. "They drop things in the water, you know, things they shouldn't."

The deer changed into a nightingale, which sang a beautiful song. Halis picked up the tune quickly and sang along. Then the nightingale became a firefly. Other fireflies joined her, emerging from the woods to dance around the nymph on the water. Halis caught one in her cupped hands, stared at it for a while to see if it was Tabitha, then released it when it was not.

When Tabitha was back on the shore again, Archibald caught her wrist. "That's enough," he said gently. "You are playing a dangerous game."

Halis watched them silently from the water, sinking down until only her eyes were above the surface.

"Why hasn't Belterras told me more about nymphs?" Tabitha asked Archibald. "Why are you here talking with one?"

"Because," he said, dismissing her second question to answer the first, "they are not creatures of this world. I expect they are one of the most powerful, most dangerous races that will ever be in your care. Nymphs, like dragons, are immortal, more like gods than animals." He paused, trying to think of a way to explain it. "If this whole world were to die tomorrow, the nymphs would not die with it. They would simply leave it and take up residence elsewhere."

Tabitha thought about that a moment, then laid back down on the rocks again. "That makes sense," she said. "Another world. I wonder if Magemothers always come from another world. Brinley came from another world too, you know." Something dawned on her and she turned to Archibald. "Oh my, Archibald, Brinley is your daughter."

"Brinley?" the nymph asked, eyes narrowing.

Tabitha nodded. "The new Magemother, she's Archibald's dau—"

"Hush, child," Archibald cut her off sharply.

"What?" Halis said, her voice rising in pitch. "What are you talking about? What of my sister? What has become of Lewilyn?"

Archibald looked at his feet, then said, "That, in part, is why I came here tonight... She is dead."

"What?" The water nymph rose out of the lake so that only her toes still touched the surface. The water bubbled and frothed around her, boiling. "MIR!" she barked, looking down at the water. "TOLARIN!"

A second later, two more nymphs rose from the lake on either side of her. The one on the left was slender, completely naked, with sharp features and eyes like an angry hawk. The one to her right wore an apron the color of blood and carried a spear made of whale bone crusted with black pearls. Archibald got to his feet nervously.

"Sisters," Halis said, "you remember Archibald."

"How could we forget?" the sharp-featured nymph said in a biting tone.

"How is our sister?" the nymph with the spear sneered. She wrinkled her nose. "Has she been a good wife to you, mortal?"

Archibald hung his head.

"She is dead," Halis told them. "He told me so."

The sisters wailed in chorus. "LIES!" The nymph with the spear pointed it at Archibald, and a giant snake tore from the water at his feet, coiling around him. Archibald grunted in surprise.

"You swore to protect her after she was taken from us," Halis accused. "You have failed."

"Wait!" Archibald shouted at them. "We have a daughter. That is what I came to tell you. She will want to meet you. She is the new Magemother."

There was a sharp intake of breath from the three nymphs.

"A child!" one said.

"That was forbidden," said another.

The nymph with the spear whispered, "Abomination." She jerked the spear like a whip in her hand. The snake lurched then, dragging Archibald into the water. He disappeared with a small gasp and the nymphs on either side of Halis dove, leaving Halis alone with Tabitha.

"We claim this man," the nymph said. "He has broken a solemn vow to us and must pay the price. Say nothing of what you have witnessed here, or you will pay the same. Follow us, and you will share his fate." With her final words, Halis slid beneath the surface.

For a moment, Tabitha gaped at the rippling water. When the ripples stilled, she sent a shout with her mind across the forest, calling Belterras.

Tabitha took to the air, unfolding her wings as a great black swan. She headed to the forest glade where they often had lessons. There was a good chance that he would be there. When she alighted on the forest floor, Belterras was waiting. She gripped the ancient mage's arm and shook it. "You have to teach me how to be a fish," she said.

"Peace," he said, attempting to calm her. "What is going on?"

"There isn't time! Anyway, I promised not to tell. I can't tell. You just have to teach me how to be a fish! I have to learn tonight!"

"Tabitha," Belterras said patiently. "We have not begun water forms yet for a reason. They are more difficult than their land-going cousins." He gestured vaguely. "Fish are subtle creatures. Their minds are ancient, simple. It takes great skill to keep your head as a fish. You cannot learn it in a single night—certainly not right now, in this state."

"I can!" she said, forcing herself to calm down. "I have to. Archibald will die if I don't."

"Archibald?" Belterras said, looking startled for the first time. "What are you talking about?" He pointed to the ground. "Tell me what's going on right this instant."

Tabitha shook her head, squeezing tears out of the corner of her eyes. "I promised him that I wouldn't say. Halis said she would kill me if I told."

"Halis?" he said softly. "The water nymph?" He covered her mouth with his hand. "No. Do not tell me. They are treacherous creatures. If you have promised them silence, then it is better that you keep it. I will teach you what you want to learn, if you will promise me that you will not take on more than you can handle alone." He looked at her meaningfully. "To break your word is forgivable, to save a life."

She nodded. "I'll be careful. I promise."

The old mage considered things, weighing the wisdom of what he was about to do, and then nodded. "Very well," he said. "Let us begin."

Hours later, with the moon high in the sky, Tabitha hopped off the bank of the lake and into the water, changing into the only fish shape that she had been able to learn in such a short amount of time: a minnow. Nervously, she swam away from the giant splash her human form had made upon entry, knowing that it might attract the attention of other fish in the lake. As a minnow, she was literally at the bottom of the food chain. She could turn back into a girl before getting swallowed, if it came to that, but only if she saw it coming.

She swam around the edge of the lake for a time, her fish eyes making the water seem brighter than it was. Eventually she gave up hope of finding the nymphs near the surface and pointed herself in the direction she knew they would be: down.

The lake was deeper than she expected, especially in the middle, and the deeper she went, the more unsavory creatures she noticed. She tried not to look at them for long and prayed they would not look at her either. Catching a brief glance of a one-eyed, shark-like fish, she hoped that if she needed to change shape again she would be able to find her way back to being a minnow before she needed to breathe; she was far too deep to reach the surface on one breath.

Just when she was sure it couldn't get any darker, she found what seemed to be the bottom. Then it shifted, rolled over beneath her, and opened its massive mouth. She tried to scream, couldn't, and then swam with all her might away from the gaping maw of the creature. The mouth slammed shut a second later, having devoured something larger and more filling than a minnow. The great fish rolled over, sucking her downward in the current of its turning body, spinning her toward the bottom of the lake before it came to rest above her, sealing her off from the surface.

From below, she realized that the creature was laying on the opening of a deep crevice, guarding it, perhaps, or just taking a nap. In any event, it was a great stroke of luck that she had gotten past it so easily. She was sure that she was going the right way now.

The sides of the lake sloped inward on all sides so that the lake narrowed into a funnel below her. She saw a pinprick of light below her and swam straight down into the neck of the funnel. As she descended, the sides of the lake came closer and closer together until she began to bump them with her fins as she swam. Finally, at the very bottom of the lake, she found the tiny opening that the light was streaming through. It was too small even for her to fit through. The opening shimmered like a waving wall of crystal glass, lit from behind with golden light. It took her a minute to figure out what it was, then she realized what it reminded her of. It looked like the surface of the water when you were swimming up from below. But that didn't make sense, did it? This surface was facing down, not up. There couldn't possibly be air on the other side of it. She wondered whether she could fit her finger through the hole if she changed back into her own shape, and before she had really decided it was a good idea, she changed back into herself again.

In her own shape, the world went utterly cold and dark. She could not see the light anymore, and she could not breathe. Panicking, she felt for where she knew the hole must be, found it, and stuck her finger through it.

The sensation she experienced next was unlike anything she had felt before; it was as if she herself had become the water and were spilling through the hole. She shook the thought out of her head and found herself lying on the floor of a cavernous golden chamber, sopping wet from head to toe, her face pressed against a large heart-shaped crystal set in a golden floor.

"Hey, you there!" a voice said. She looked up to see a thin boy running at her. He was dressed in plain woolen clothes that were several sizes too big for him. There was a shock of white in his blond hair, though he could hardly be older than she was. He was carrying an open book that looked too heavy for him, the pages flapping frantically to and fro. "What are you doing?" he demanded, slamming the book shut so that he could run more easily. "How did you get in here?"

"I came through the lake," she said, her voice echoing around the massive chamber, "down a big funnel thing, and then. . ." She waved her hand in a nondescript way as she rose to her feet. "I was here."

The boy came to a stop in front of her and tilted his head back, looking up. She followed his gaze to a point several hundred feet above them where the ceiling dipped down on all sides like the outside of a funnel. Maybe it was the light playing tricks on her, but she thought she could see a tiny droplet of water in the center of it.

"The lake?"

"Yes," she said. "The lake. Now, where is Archibald? I've come to take him back. You can't kill him. You just simply can't. He's too decent, and he's my friend."

The boy gawked at her. "Are you talking about the prisoner that the three queens brought down?"

"I expect so," Tabitha said tentatively. "Yes. Three queens?" She thought back on Halis's words, trying to remember if the three nymphs were supposed to be queens.

The boy raised his hand, ticking off fingers one by one. "Halis, Mir, Tolarin. The three queens of Nymia."

"Queens of what?" she said, taking off her socks and wringing them out on the floor.

"Don't—oh, never mind. I'll have to clean it up anyway. Nymia. You know, the nymph kingdom. I believe you now, that you came from the lake."

"What do you mean?" she said, grimacing as she struggled to pull the sodden socks back onto her already cold feet.

"Well," the boy said, "you're either telling the truth and you're not from here, or you're the stupidest person in all of Nymia."

Tabitha rounded on him. "I am not!"

"I know," he said, holding up his hands. "That's what I said. I just don't know how you got in here. The portal is supposed to be guarded."

"Well," Tabitha said, "the guard was hungry."

"What? Oh, never mind. You know, nobody has ever gotten in here before." He scratched his head. "I don't even remember what protocol is." His face went white. "I expect you've broken several laws already. You'll have to answer to the queen."

"Which one?"

The boy frowned. "I don't know. Halis, hopefully, otherwise you're doomed. Mir and Tolarin don't like aliens."

Tabitha laughed.

"What?"

"You called me an alien."

The boy went red in the face. "Well, you're not from here, are you?"

She shook her head, swallowing a stray chuckle.

"Then you're an alien, and you'll have to go before the queen."

Tabitha smiled. "I don't think so," she said, shifting suddenly. A great black swan took flight from where she had been standing.

"AAAGH! Sorcery!" the boy shouted, twisting and slipping in the puddle that she had left, falling onto his backside.

Tabitha flew to the opposite side of the massive circular hall. There was a large golden archway there, then it was gone. She hovered in front of the bare stretch of wall where the archway had been moments before and then turned around. There it was, off to her left.

Again, as soon as she approached it, the archway vanished. Puzzled, Tabitha turned again, spotting the archway on the opposite end of the room. She flew toward it, only slightly hopeful this time, and banked before she collided with solid stone. She landed at the feet of the boy with the book, who had made his way to a round desk covered in books and shiny silver buttons. A large, very dusty hammer sat on the only portion of the desk not covered in books. "There's no way out," she said breathlessly.

"I know."

Tabitha sniffed. Most likely there was a way out, and this boy knew it. "What's your name again?"

The boy squared his shoulders, taking a deep breath. "Fitzpatrick Auldo Waltverian McYormic the Third...but you may call me Fitz, so long as you stop making puddles on my floor and flying around the room."

"Sorry," she said. "Will you help me leave now? I really do need to find Archibald, you know..."

"No." He turned his back to her, fiddling with the buttons on his desk. "You're an intruder, like I said. An alien. I have to sound the alarm, as soon as I figure out how to do it." He punched an especially large button several times, looking around, then frowned at it when nothing happened. "Bother."

Tabitha leaned against the desk to watch him. "Are you a guard?" she asked.

He glanced up, startled. "Oh, no. I mean—well, yes, sort of."

Tabitha raised her eyebrows and the boy coughed. He folded his arms, leaning casually against the desk and pushing several buttons by accident, which caused him to say "Bother," again. "Technically, I'm the gatekeeper," he explained. "But to be honest, I don't have much to do. Nobody ever comes here. Halis used to go out and visit people in Aberdeen all the time, but even she hasn't been here in years." His eyes went wide. "Then she just showed up randomly today, and then the other queens came too, and then they came back with the alien."

"Don't call him that," Tabitha said. "He's the trusted advisor to the King of Aberdeen, and my friend."

"Sorry," he said. "I don't mean anything by it. I've just been here too long. Actually, I'm an alien too, I guess."

Tabitha brightened. "Really? You mean you're from Aberdeen?"

The boy nodded. "I was a student at the Magisterium, if you know what that is. I don't know if it's even there anymore."

Tabitha laughed. "Of course it is! Oh, this is wonderful. I am a student there too—I mean, I was, until I became the Magemother's Herald—and now I'm Belterras's apprentice too, so I'll never really be a student there again. I was their bird keeper," she finished proudly. Her mood had brightened considerably at the revelation that she was speaking to a fellow student. "When did you attend the school?"

"Long ago." He smiled weakly. "Before there was a bird keeper. I started there the year the school opened."

Tabitha stared at him blankly. Her eyes glazed over. Fitz waved a hand in front of her face and she snapped back. "Oh! Sorry. But you must be ancient. I mean, you must be over five hundred years old!"

Fitz looked down at his hands despondently. "So then, time has passed there," he said quietly.

"Oh, yes, lots."

He nodded. "I figured as much."

"What's wrong?" Tabitha asked, for his eyes had started to water. "What did I say?"

"Well," he said, pointing around the room. "Time does not exist in here, or so I've read. I didn't know how long I've been in here...Time enough to read all these books a hundred times." He waved a hand at the stacks of thick tomes. "But I didn't really know until just now. Everyone I knew in Aberdeen is dead now."

Tabitha gasped, putting a hand over her mouth. "Oh no! You're right! But Fitz, how did you get here in the first place?"

"It's a long story," he said.

Tabitha cleared off a pile of books, sat down on the desk beside him, and picked up his hand in her own, which made him go bright red in the face. "Maybe you can tell me," she said, "before you sound the alarm. After all, it sounds like it might be a long time before you see someone else again." Tabitha hoped that this was the right thing to do. Part of her wanted to hurry up and figure out a way to get out of there. So much time had already passed since Archibald was taken. He might be in very great danger, or it might be too late already. But another part of her was certain that the only way out of this room was Fitz, who seemed like he needed a friend at the moment.

Fitz blinked at her thoughtfully, then shrugged and settled down onto a stack of books, the top-most volume of which was so concave that Tabitha could tell he had been using it as a chair for a long time.

"It started when I was a student at the school," Fitz began. "I was good at my classes, but my books were my only friends. My classmates had friends, best friends, girlfriends, all kinds of friends, but not me."

Tabitha felt a twinge of pain listening to him. He could have been describing her own life back at the school, where she had spent most of her time up in the bird tower, talking to birds instead of people.

"One day, quite by accident, I met Halis by the underground river beneath the Magisterium. I used to go there sometimes just to be alone. I mean, it wasn't really an accident. I was trying to summon a nymph. I had read about how to do it, but I didn't think it would actually work—I was just doing it because I was bored. But it did work." He paused, remembering. "She said she had never spoken to a boy before. Anyway, she knew a lot of things about uh…girls." He blushed. "She gave me advice, and in return I gave her news about the world, but she got bored with that pretty soon. She had all kinds of questions for me about the Magisterium and magic and how it worked. Eventually I brought her a book to read. She didn't know how, so I taught her."

"You taught the queen of the nymphs to read?" Tabitha asked, impressed.

"Worst thing I ever did," he said, nodding. "The more she read, the more she wanted to read. Soon I was stealing two or three books a day for her from the library. Of course, someone noticed and I got in trouble. They said they would throw me out if I didn't return the books, so I asked Halis to give them back, and she said no."

"But that's not fair," Tabitha objected. "You were nice to her."

Fitz smiled weakly. "It gets worse. She said she wanted more books. She said she was going to put me in prison if I didn't get her more, but I couldn't, so..." He waved a hand at the expansive chamber they sat in. "Here I am."

"Your prison," Tabitha echoed, looking around the room with a new curiosity.

"Of sorts. I'm left to myself here, keeping guard over the gate to a fairy kingdom that I have never set foot inside, getting older and older every day, though it never shows. These are all the books I gave her," he said, indicating the mountain of books with a wry smile. "They have been my only companions."

Tabitha's eyes widened. "That's terrible. And you've read them all?"

Fitz laughed bitterly. "I have become, through my own studies, a pretty decent wizard, if I do say so myself." Fitz stood up, stretching. "Well, that's my story. I suppose now I need to deal with you." He frowned at the metal buttons, pushing several of them again with no success. "I don't know why these aren't working," he said. "I guess we will just have to wait until someone checks in on us."

Tabitha stirred. "But that could be another five hundred years!" she said. "I can't wait that long. Archibald is in danger right now!"

Fitz shrugged. "There is no way for a mortal to leave this room alive," he said simply. "If there were, I would have done it ages ago."

"But how did Halis and the other queens come in here?" Tabitha asked.

Fitz pointed to the wall on the opposite end of the room. "Oh, there's a gate. A big golden gate under a golden archway. But mortals can't walk through it. It won't appear for us. Sometimes you can get a glimpse of it, but that's all. Only the nymphs can use it." He frowned, glancing around suspiciously. "It always seems to be moving, too. I probably spent my whole first month chasing it, but it's no use. Trust me."

"There has to be a way to get out," Tabitha insisted. "I can't just let Archibald die."

"Oh, there's a way," Fitz said darkly. "I didn't say there was no way out. I said there was no way out alive."

"What do you mean?"

Fitz pointed to the giant glass heart set into the floor. "That's the Queen's Heart," he said, sliding a small manual out from beneath a stack of books. The cover read "Book of Laws." He opened to the middle and began to read. "The penalty for entering Nymia is death. No mortal who enters the Golden Hall—that's this room—shall live to tell about it, though the brave at heart may win a quick death, and an audience with the queen, by ringing the Queen's Heart." Fitz snapped the book shut with a sense of finality. "So you see, the only way out is to take the hammer." He pointed to the large dusty hammer on the desk. "And ring the heart. It will get you an audience with the queen, but then you get executed." He glanced down at the book and made a face. "If I remember right, it's not a very pretty kind of execution either, so I wouldn't recommend—Hey! Wait!"

Tabitha, who had stopped listening after he finished explaining about the heart, was halfway across to it, hammer in hand.

"DON'T DO IT!" Fitz cried, running after her. "I didn't finish telling you about the—"

Whatever he was about to say was cut off by a sound like a giant drum as Tabitha brought the hammer down on the center of the heart. It was a good swing. She had been careful to raise the hammer high above her head and bend her elbows on the downswing like Master Bumps had taught her all those years ago when she was learning how to cut firewood to heat the bird tower. The sound that came from it was not what she had been expecting. It wasn't at all like you would expect metal on glass to sound like. It sounded instead like a very big heartbeat: two big thumps a half second apart. She dropped the hammer in surprise.

"Now you've done it," Fitz said, catching up to her. There was a look in his eyes that was half fear, half admiration. "You shouldn't have done that. I didn't finish telling you about what happens."

"It doesn't matter," Tabitha said. "I have to see the queen. I have to save Archibald."

"But you don't understand," Fitz insisted. "It's not that easy."

Tabitha turned to him. "What do you mean? You said if I rang it I'd get to see the queen, and that's what I did."

His response was cut off by a clanging sound from behind them. There, at the end of the room, the golden arch had appeared. The gate beneath it had swung open and two very strong-looking men were striding towards them. They wore armor and carried spears, and the skin beneath their helmets was blue like Halis and the other nymphs.

Tabitha expected one of the nymph soldiers to shout, "Who struck the Queen's Heart?" but nothing like that happened. They strode up to them quietly, somberly. The soldier closest to her took the hammer from her hands and handed it to Fitz. "The penalty for what you have done is death," he said softly. "If you are worthy, you will speak with the queen before you die."

"If I'm worthy?"

The soldier said nothing, just took her upper arm in a firm grip and began leading her towards the gate.

"Wait," she said. "What about Fitz? He made me do it!"

The soldier stopped to look at Fitz questioningly. Fitz had gone white as a sheet. Standing there next to the heart, hammer in hand, he looked very guilty. "I did not!" he protested. "I just told her the options. I was just doing my job."

"Should an intruder enter," the soldier next to Tabitha said to Fitz, "you are only permitted to read to them out of the Book of Laws. Then they are to be left to make their own decisions."

"That's what I did!" Fitz exclaimed. "I mean, I did talk to her, but I read to her, too." He waved the hammer in front of himself, so flustered now that his arm shook nervously. "You can't expect me not to talk at all after not seeing another person for so long."

As Tabitha watched, Fitz's nervous shaking got worse. On top of the shaking, Fitz had started to sweat. Tabitha remembered what he had said about his difficulty speaking to others, and of his shyness. No doubt being locked up alone for five hundred years had not helped matters.

The soldier considered him. "We will report your behavior to the Council of the Three Queens, and you will be punished as they see fit."

"No, don't!" Fitz shouted, stepping forward so that he stood directly over the heart. "I promise I won't do it agai—"

But on his last word, Fitz shook so badly that the heavy hammer slipped from his hand and fell on the heart.

Tabitha covered her ears again as it thumped loudly.

When it was over, the soldiers were both staring at Fitz with livid, surprised expressions, and soon he was being led out of the room alongside her.

"Why did you say that?" Fitz hissed at her. "You made them question me, and I got so...so—"

Tabitha put a hand on his arm as they walked toward the gate. "You're welcome," she said. "You've been locked in here too long, Fitz. Don't worry," she added. "We're going to be fine."

"I doubt that."

Tabitha, hoping he was wrong, grabbed his hand as they walked beneath the golden gate into the darkness beyond.

Part Two

In which there is a dragon

THE DARKNESS BEYOND the gate was the inside of a tunnel, which, after a few minutes, opened to the strangest view that Tabitha had ever seen. They were on a beach, but it was unlike any beach that she had seen before; the brown earth beneath their feet was so dark that she would have taken it for black had it not been for the water running up against it. The water was blacker than the deepest darkness of night shadows, blacker than the bottom of a well and the space between stars.

The water was evil, she sensed. It must be; nothing but evil could be so black. She knew right away that she didn't want to touch it. As soon as she had the thought, the water seemed to creep toward her across the ground. She shied away from it nervously. Above them, the sky was a deep crimson red. Tabitha took it all in silently. Red sky over a twisting coast of brown earth and an ocean of black. It was not the beautiful kingdom that she'd imagined. This was a harsh place. In the emptiness of the ocean, her eyes were drawn toward the only object in it: a small raft, bobbing up and down on the water. She knew instantly, horribly, that they would have to get on it.

The soldiers waited as they climbed onto it carefully.

"Do not touch the water," one of them warned needlessly. Then he put his armored foot on the edge of the raft and pushed them out to sea. The other soldier tossed a small oar to them and Fitz caught it.

"Wait!" Tabitha called to them. "Aren't you coming?" But the soldiers just smiled at her through their helmets. A second later they were gone, vanishing from the beach like smoke in the wind.

"Where did they go?" Tabitha asked. "What's going on?"

Fitz sat down silently on the back of the raft and began to paddle, first on one side, then on the other. "To see the queen," he said, "you have to pass a test. That's what I was trying to tell you before you rang the heart."

"What kind of test?" Tabitha said, sitting down unsteadily and trying not to think of the black death beneath them.

"The hardest kind," Fitz said darkly. He removed his hands from the oar, and it continued to paddle by itself. He folded his arms glumly. He closed his eyes as if trying to remember. "The Book of Laws states that it is a journey through the darkness of your own soul."

Tabitha's face went blank, staring off the edge of the raft into the calmly undulating blackness.

"Tabitha?"

"Oh," she said, coming back to herself. "Right. Darkness of my soul. Well, that doesn't sound too bad. I'm not a very dark person. Are you?"

Fitz frowned but said nothing.

"Are you afraid?" Tabitha asked him.

He shrugged. "I didn't mean to ring the bell. You did. I think this is going to be your journey. I'm just along for the ride."

A wave lifted them several feet into the air and Tabitha's eyes went wide in panic. "Oh!" she squawked. "I hate the ocean."

Fitz grimaced. "That explains why it is here, then."

"What do you mean?"

"Don't you get it?" he said angrily. "Until we meet the queen—if we meet the queen—everything we see, everything we experience, is going to be because of you. This is a journey through the darkness of your soul. Your fears, your deep dark secrets, that's what we're going to face. That's the test."

"But I don't have any secrets!" Tabitha objected. Her voice caught on the last word as she felt something shift in the back of her mind like a restless animal. Suddenly, she felt afraid.

"Look!" Fitz said. "There's something there!"

It looked like an island in the water, far enough away that she could not tell how big it was. She felt hopeful at the sight of it, glad at the thought of getting out of the water. They paddled toward it for what must have been an hour, but it didn't seem to get any closer. After three hours, they had nearly given up hope.

"Maybe a current will catch us eventually," Fitz mumbled, stretching out to rest.

Wind caught Tabitha's hair and tossed it, making her look around. Thick clouds had gathered in the crimson sky, dark and menacing, shaped like anvils and towers and saddles and other things that clouds should not be shaped like when you are on a tiny raft in the ocean.

"Oh no," she breathed. The wind picked up and the smooth water beneath them started to swell. Soon they were riding waves up and down. It felt like they were on a sled, racing over hills of black snow. Every moment a new hill would rise in front of them and they would climb it, then Tabitha would grab hold of the raft and try not to scream as they slid down the other side.

"This is going to get worse," Fitz warned. As if responding to his words, lightning lanced across the red sky and the corner of their raft dipped into the ocean. Tabitha watched, horrified, unable to move as black water slid over the surface of the raft like quicksilver, brushing her hand.

When it touched her, she felt more afraid than she ever had before, though she couldn't think why. It was just water, after all. Wasn't it?

"Look!" Fitz shouted, pulling her from her fearful thoughts. "The storm is pushing us towards it!"

Tabitha glanced up to see the island, much larger now, hovering before them in the water. "Will we get there in time?" she called as the wind began to howl. His answer was drowned out by a wave of thunder. A few drops of water followed it, black and cold as the ocean beneath them. Then few became many, and in a moment, they were soaked through.

Tabitha couldn't see the island anymore. She couldn't see the ocean beneath them, but she knew it was there. She had lost track of which way was up, but she could still breathe, so she knew she must not be underwater. The wind was screaming now, and she couldn't hear Fitz. Her stomach lurched as they tipped over the top of a wave. She screamed without hearing it, her head smacking into the wood of the raft as they skidded down the water on the other side. She kicked out wildly, looking for Fitz with her feet, and connected with something soft. His stomach, she thought, or his face maybe. Good, at least she wasn't totally alone.

She was wet to the bone, frozen stiff. Her fingers were screaming at her through the cold, begging her to let go and fall into the waves. She considered it briefly, and then the choice was taken from her as the raft corkscrewed off the end of a violent wave and sent her careening into the cold, frothing dark.

She felt fear then, worse than before. She had felt fear in her heart before, at the thought of being alone forever. She had felt fear in her stomach too, when she tripped down the stairs in the dark and thought she had broken her leg. Now she felt fear with her whole body—everywhere the water touched, springing out of her skin, her hair, her throat. She swallowed it, choking on death itself.

Then her hands briefly touched something firm. The water pulled her away from it, and she clawed at it fruitlessly. A second later a wave sent her back and her hands touched it again, her face, her body. She had reached the island. Somehow she got her feet beneath her and ran until the waves and the wind and the rain was gone.

She collapsed beneath the shelter of a stone arch at the edge of a dark city. Fitz was there, waiting for her in the shadows, looking wet and cold and terrified, as if death itself had shaken his hand. After what she'd just been through, it probably had.

"What else are you afraid of?" he whispered.

"I don't know."

He gave her a half smile. "Well, I guess we're about to find out."

They rested for a while, then finally, because it was the only thing to do, Tabitha pushed herself to her feet and walked into the dark city. Fitz followed her. They passed under a low city gate and turned randomly, haphazardly down streets lined with dark houses squashed together like too many peas jammed into one pod. Presently, they rounded a corner and caught sight of a column of smoke trailing from the narrow black chimney of a bedraggled-looking inn. They stood at the edge of a wide, empty square. The moon was high in the black sky, and the only sign of life in the city was an ancient looking hag wrapped in black rags, who had settled herself awkwardly in the middle of the square with her legs jutting out from under her at odd angles, as if they were too old to fold properly.

"Oh!" Tabitha said. "I know where we are!" The fear had fallen from her face, replaced with a look of wonder.

"Where?" Fitz asked, but she didn't answer.

They walked toward the old woman, their feet echoing softly beneath them. She had a small black bowl and was spreading birdseed on the ground around her. Most of the birds were asleep, of course, but occasionally some nocturnal creature would idle down from a nearby eave and sample her wares.

"Wayla," Tabitha said pleasantly, sitting down next to the old woman, "I can't believe you're still here."

"Leave me be," the woman croaked. "I'm not makin' any trouble. Mindin' my own business, I am."

Tabitha paid her no mind. She picked up some birdseed and held it in her upraised hand, calling to the birds, waking them from their small dreams. They came to her, Jay and Sparrow and Dove, and emptied her hand. The woman turned a wondering eye on her, whispering, "Not a waste, then, I see." Then she vanished.

Fitz let out a little involuntary shout and stamped his foot around on the stones where the old woman had been a second before. "Is she a witch? I don't like witches," he declared. "Are you afraid of witches?"

She shook her head. "I don't think she's a witch. I don't know what she is. She's just Wayla. She's been here feeding the birds at night since I was little. I grew up here," she explained, remembering that she hadn't told him.

"Here?" he said, looking around for some explanation of where here was. "Here where?"

"Hesh," she said. "By the sea. I haven't been here since..." The shadow of a dark memory fell across her face. She shook it away and said, "What is Hesh doing in the nymph kingdom?"

Fitz rubbed his eyes wearily. "It isn't real. It's part of the test." He looked around at the buildings, the cobwebs shining in the moonlight, stretching between the close-set houses. A mouse ran out of a drain in the square and picked at the birdseed. "Sure looks real, though."

Voices fell over them from across the square. Three people, two adults and a child, moved toward them without seeing them. A mother and a father, each holding their daughter's hand. The child said something, pointing at a bird landing in the square, and the father laughed.

"No," Tabitha said softly, rising.

"What?"

"We can't be here. This isn't real."

"What can't be? What's going on, Tabitha? Who are those people?"

Tabitha had her hands over her mouth. She was backing away, trying to turn around, trying to run, but her eyes were glued on the people walking towards them.

A man leaped from the shadows at the people on the other side of the square. He was dressed in black, a long knife flashing in his hand. The father reached for him, slipped on something wet on the ground—wash water, a rotten tomato, he would never know—and fell beneath the knife. The woman screamed, "Tabitha!"

Fitz turned to see Tabitha running, her back to the screaming woman and the little girl and the man with the knife. He followed her.

"What was that?" he asked her, when she stopped. She had reached the sea and could run no further. She shook her head, unwilling to put a name to it, but he had already guessed. "Was that you?" he said. "A memory? Your family? The woman screamed your name before...before..." He hadn't seen it, but he knew what had happened.

Tabitha wasn't listening. She had that faraway look in her eyes again, like she was someplace else. A tear streaked down her face and her expression changed, darkened. She wore rage like a mask—one that she had never worn before. She walked down the shore until the black water covered her feet.

"What are you doing?" Fitz cried, but it was too late. She dove into the ocean, swimming madly, not out, but down, looking for something in the darkness, something born of pain and fear and need. She knew it would be there, waiting for her; it always had been.

Fitz watched the water, waiting, then fell backwards, shielding his eyes as something massive burst from the waves, sprinkling the shore with water. Each drop pricked his skin with ice cold fear. Fear rose out of the water too; he had no other name for it. A great menacing creature, black as the ocean, dripped darkness and fire over the shore, its great wings pounding him flat against the sand with air, its eyes the color of Tabitha's. It soared over the city wall and banked toward the square. Fitz ran after it. He heard the dragon bellow, heard flame issuing from its mouth, heard jaws snapping and a man's high, wild cry. Then he heard nothing.

When he made it to the square, the man in black was gone. The father and mother lay on the ground. Tabitha was walking across the square holding the younger girl's hand, talking to her in soft tones. She took her to Wayla, the old woman, who had reappeared amid her circle of birdseed, and the older Tabitha, hands shaking, handed her younger self over to the woman.

"I'll take her to the wizard's school," Wayla said. "They'll find a place for her."

"I know."

Wayla turned the girl's head away from her fallen parents and led her out of the square, then everything, the square, the city, Wayla, and the small Tabitha, disappeared. They were alone in the ocean again, on the little raft under the stars.

"I'm sorry," Fitz said, putting a hand on her shoulder.

She turned to him, searching his face, his eyes. Tears filled her own. She put her face on his chest. "Why did I do that?" she asked. "Why did you let me?"

"It's what I would have done," he said. "He deserved it."

"I'm just like him," she sobbed. "Just like him now!" She beat his chest with her fist.

"Tabitha!" He shook her, making the raft rock beneath them. "This is all just a dream! Just a dream!"

She came out of his arms, blinking. "Just a dream," she muttered. "I forgot...it seems so real. Did I fail the test?"

He shook his head. "I don't think it's that simple. Anyway, it's not over yet." He pointed at something ahead of them and she followed his finger. The ocean disappeared before them, just stopped in a dark line, beyond which nothing was visible. A sound like thunder issued from the place the water disappeared and it took her a moment to realize what it was. "Hold on," Fitz said, taking her in his arms. They were speeding towards it now, the largest waterfall she had ever seen. "We can't die. It's just a dream," he assured her.

"Just a dream," she repeated, her voice rising as their raft tipped over the edge. They plummeted fifty, a hundred, two hundred feet, falling away from the raft, from each other. Vaguely, Tabitha remembered that she could fly. She had done it before. She could take the shape of a bird, if she wished. She could have wings. Suddenly she remembered the other thing that she could become, that she had become, wings and wrath and rage, and she dared not become any flying thing. What if she tried to shape a sparrow and the dragon broke out of her instead? She could feel it in her still, like a memory she couldn't get rid of. She didn't want to risk becoming that monster again, no matter what the cost, so she pushed all thought of escape out of her mind and fell.

Part Three

In which there is an empty throne

AFTER A FALL THAT SEEMED LIKE FOREVER, Tabitha hit water and swore she heard every bone in her body break. A hand pulled her toward air and she coughed, letting it fill her. "This dream hurts," she mumbled, and she heard Fitz laugh.

"Cheer up," he said. "Look where we are."

She did, and it made her smile. Their raft had followed the water to where it emptied into a world of wildflowers. Everything was flowers here, she knew; there was nothing more to be afraid of. Hills rolled away from them as far as they could see, each one crowned with wildflowers of a different brilliant hue—red, blue, green, gold. Birds chirped happily, dancing through the sky, chasing each other around lilies tall as trees. A bright pink sky twinkled down at them warmly, strewn with daytime starlight.

"What is this place?" Fitz breathed.

Tabitha smiled in spite of herself. "I don't know." It looked familiar. It felt like home. It made something deep inside her relax. But she knew that she had never been there before, except perhaps in forgotten dreams.

Something walked out of the flowers before them, purple and blue and gold parting in its wake. It was the most beautiful creature she had ever seen. It had a lion's body and an eagle's wings and a face that she knew would always live in her heart.

"Peridot!" she cried, and ran to embrace her.

"Tabitha," Peridot said, pulling her into a hug with a great lion's paw. "You have come."

"Have you been waiting for me? I'm sorry. I didn't know!" She turned to Fitz, who was staring at his feet like he shouldn't be there. "Fitz," she said, "this is Peridot. She was the old Magemother's Herald. Isn't this lovely? But, Peridot!" she said, remembering. "You died!"

"Yes," the winged lion said, her voice calm. She leaned in until their eyes almost touched. "Now you protect the Magemother."

Tabitha covered her mouth, averting her eyes, staring at the flowers. "That's right," she whispered. "Why did she pick me?"

Peridot's eyes softened. "She picked you because she sees in you what you do not. Not yet, at least," she added.

Tabitha reached out to touch the lion's face, then brought her hand back and held her arms close, like a wounded thing. She whispered, "I don't want to be the Magemother's Herald anymore, Peridot. I can't."

"I know," Peridot said. Her eyes gleamed in the rose-tinted light. "That is why I am here."

"I can't protect her. I can't fight. I can't hurt things." She thought of the man lunging at her parents with a knife, saw herself rising out the black water, terrible, carrying death between her wings like a chain. She shuddered. "I can't be...what she needs me to be."

Peridot lifted her head and turned away. "Then she will die."

Tabitha sunk to her knees, buried her face in her hands. "I'm sorry," she said.

Peridot roared.

Tabitha peeked over her hands to see the great lion leap into the air. Peridot flapped her wings once, twice, then landed beside Fitz, knocking him to the ground with a swipe of her paw. Fitz was trembling.

"Will you let me kill him?" Peridot asked, turning to look at her calmly. "Will you let me kill your friend as you will let them kill the Magemother?"

Tabitha leaped to her feet. "She's my friend, too," she said viciously. "And so is Fitz. Peridot, stop!"

Peridot looked back at Fitz, stepping toward him as he scurried across the ground, backing away from her. "He means nothing to me," she said flatly. She sniffed the air above him. "He is old. Too old to look so young. He has lived his life. You stop me."

"But why?" Tabitha pleaded. "This isn't like you." She glanced from side to side, putting her hands to her head. "This isn't real," she whispered. "It's just a dream."

Peridot brushed Fitz's scrambling legs with a claw, tearing them open. Fitz screamed. Peridot roared, her face going wild, and Fitz blanched. "YOU ARE THE MAGEMOTHER'S HERALD!" she roared at Tabitha. "PROTECT HIM!" She leaped into the air, flapping her wings once, twice, gaining height, then she twisted around, spinning toward Fitz, fangs bared, paws reaching for him.

The dragon's claws swatted her out of the air.

Peridot landed like a spring on the meadow floor, leaped skyward and streaked around Tabitha, dragging razor sharp claws across her scales, tearing at the soft membrane of her wing. "YES!" she roared. "GOOD!"

Tabitha roared too, pushing herself skyward, away from lion's claws and fangs. Peridot circled her long serpentine body as she rose, darting away from her claws with expert grace.

Tabitha let fire pour out of her, bathing them both in red.

Peridot cried out, her wings catching fire, feathers burning, eyes blinded. She fell through the air toward the flowers. The dragon caught her before she fell too far, lowering her gently to the ground. She sniffed the lion's scorched fur, looking for life and, finding none, groaned. The damage was done.

Tabitha stood alone in her own form again, staring at what she had done. Then, to her surprise, the lion's body flickered and faded, like shadows at dawn, into nothing.

She heard a twig snap behind her, the rustle of flowers parting, and turned to see a living, vibrant Peridot stepping out of the azure petals.

"Peridot," she said, dumbfounded.

"You see," Peridot said smiling. "You have it in you. Here." She touched Tabitha's heart with a claw. "The fierceness that is needed."

"I killed you," Tabitha whispered.

Peridot sighed. "Death," she said, "is a thing that you should not fear so much. It is like a shadow—dark, mysterious, but hardly real. In the end there is only life."

"But you're dead," Tabitha said numbly.

"Am I? How would you know?"

Tabitha shook her head, confused. "No. I don't know."

Peridot smiled, then sat down beside her. "When you fight for the Magemother," she said, "it matters not what you must do, but why you do it. How you do it. You can fight to protect the light. You can use violence and you will not become the darkness. But only if you do it out of love, out of duty, and always out of absolute necessity. Ferocity is not a bad thing, anymore than a sword is a bad thing, or a rock. It is how you use it, and why, that separates the good and bad."

Tabitha wiped a tear from her cheek and sniffed. "I don't like it," she whispered. "The part of me that can do that. It scares me."

Peridot nodded. "That is one reason the Magemother chose you." She got to her feet, stretched her wings at her sides, and folded them in again. "Now," she said, "let us go and heal your friend."

"Fitz!" Tabitha exclaimed, rushing to his side as she remembered. He was unconscious, his leg torn and bleeding badly into the earth. "How do we heal him?" she said desperately.

"Love," the lion said. "And perhaps a touch of remorse."

"Your remorse?" Tabitha asked.

Peridot looked at her intently. "No, child, yours, for dragging him into this. This is your world, remember? Your dream. Everything in it is your doing." She smiled warmly, confidently, and began to fade into the warm air like mist. "Heal him," she whispered. And then she was gone.

Tabitha turned back to Fitz, taking his head in her hands, touching his leg. "I'm sorry," she said. "I didn't mean to hurt you. It's all my fault!" She thought of the fear that had held her—the fear of hurting people—and how it had made her hurt him. She remembered the rage of the dragon, its power, and became a dragon again, white this time instead of black. She felt love fill her heart, compassion instead of rage, felt it flow out of her as fire. She bathed him in golden flames, bright as her love, warm as their friendship, and he stirred.

She shivered, becoming herself again, and took his hand in hers. "Thank you for coming back to me," she said.

He groaned. "Is your dream over yet?"

She looked around curiously. "Yes," she said. "I think so."

At her words, the world around them changed. The sky darkened, the earth became water, filling up the space around them. The flowers became people, a great silent crowd of people watching her, their skin as blue as the water they lived in, their faces shining. Her breath caught in her throat as her mouth filled with water. She couldn't breathe here, she realized. Then she felt a hand grab her own. Fitz squeezed her fingers, touched her lips, and she breathed air again.

"Thanks," she said, not pausing to wonder how he had done it; the crowd was parting before them, revealing four silver thrones upon a raised dais, three with queens in them, one empty.

Tabitha and Fitz, hand in hand, crossed the distance to stand before them.

Halis spoke first. She sat on the right, next to the empty throne. "You are a strange and wonderful creature, Tabitha."

"Dangerous," one of the other queens said. Tabitha recognized her from their meeting earlier on the surface of the lake. She no longer wore her red apron, but her spear was laid across her lap.

"Yes," Halis said, "that too."

She lifted a hand and Archibald stepped out from behind her throne. "I believe this is who you came for."

"Archibald!"

Archibald strode down the steps as if he hadn't a care in the world, smiling warmly. He said, "You did well." He didn't look at all like a person who had been abducted and condemned to death.

"What's going on, Archibald?"

Archibald placed a hand on her shoulder. "They needed to test you, to get to know you and see if they could trust you, see if they could respect you as the Mage of Earth someday." He glanced back at the dais out of the corner of his eye. "They have their own ways of doing things here."

"So you weren't really kidnapped?" she asked numbly. "This was all for nothing?"

Halis stood from her place on the dais. "No, Tabitha," she said. "This was the gravest of challenges, the most serious in nature." She glanced around at the crowd of onlookers. "Nymphs are not rabbits or squirrels. We do not simply accept the passing of one Mage and the appearance of another. We do not give care of our world blindly into the hands of a stranger. Nymphs," she emphasized, "are suspicious by nature. Our past has taught us to be cautious."

"You can say that again," Archibald mumbled.

"Belterras informed us of your apprenticeship to him and asked us to test you," she said. "Though I don't think he expected us to do so for some time," she admitted. She folded her arms and sat down. "But the test is best performed when you are not expecting it. Take heart," she added at the look of worry on Tabitha's face. "You did well." She motioned towards the queen with the spear on her lap and said, "This is my sister, Tolarin."

Tolarin nodded curtly. "Everything you experienced today since entering our world has been a test of your nature. It has revealed many things to us." The spear twitched on her lap as she paused. "We have seen your darkest memory, the brutal murder of your parents when you were a child."

"I am Mir," the third queen said. Her narrow, grave features held something that Tabitha didn't recognize, something between fascination and mild dislike. "We have seen how your darkest memory gave birth to your deepest fear: the fear of violence. The fear of becoming that which you hate."

"We have also seen your greatest strength," Halis said, "which is your love. You will lay aside your fears to save your friends. We have seen your heart itself . . . a beautiful country." She gave a formal nod. "You have won our trust and our friendship, and you are permitted to leave here with Archibald and return to your world. When the day comes that you become the Mage of Earth, we will follow you." She raised a hand. "Our gift to you is the test itself, for we have given you a great knowledge. To know yourself is the foremost mystery of life, to find yourself, the critical discovery. Use it well."

Tabitha gave what she thought was a grateful sort of bow. "I will. Thank you. But . . ." She looked at the boy beside her. "What about Fitz? Won't you let him go, too? He helped me, and he's my friend. Doesn't that count for something?"

Halis smiled. "Fitz will not leave with you," she said. "But do not worry for him. Fitz was a part of your test." She rolled her hand gracefully toward Fitz and he shimmered and shifted around the edges as the flowers had done, growing taller, leaner, his skin turning blue. "This is my son," she said. "He agreed to help us with your test."

Fitz lifted Tabitha's hand and brushed it lightly with his lips. "I'm sorry," he said. Tabitha yanked her hand out of his, blinking at him in surprise. His eyes, at least, were still the same. "Come with me," he said, gesturing to the empty throne. She followed him. "Sit," he said.

She shook her head.

"Sit," Halis repeated, moving beside her. The other queens had left their thrones too. They were standing beside her, waiting for her to sit. She did.

"I don't understand," Tabitha said.

"This is the other reason we brought you here," Halis said. "To sit on the empty throne."

"It is not yours," Tolarin said, noting the question on Tabitha's face.

"It belongs to our sister," Mir said.

Halis nodded. "To Lewilyn."

"Brinley's mother," Tabitha whispered.

"Yes," Halis said. "Once she filled it. Once she reigned with us in glory and happiness, but she was taken from us."

"You want her back," Tabitha guessed. Her voice grew soft, tentative. "But she died."

"No," Tolarin said. "We do not want her back. It was her choice to leave."

"And no," Mir added. "She is not dead."

Tabitha looked at her questioningly.

"She is our sister," Halis said. "We would know if she died. She has not."

"We brought you here," Tolarin said, resting the sharp blade of her spear on Tabitha's thigh to get her attention, "so that you could see her beginnings, her roots. We sit you on her empty throne so that you will remember."

"We did not give up a queen and a sister to see her forgotten by your world, lost to a half-death, unexplained."

Tolarin lifted the spear to Tabitha's chest and there was cold certainty in her eyes. "You will find her."

Halis touched the spear, pushing it away. "That is our charge to you," she said. "That is the first thing you will do for us as the future Mage of Earth. This you must do for us to keep our trust."

Tolarin brought the butt of the spear down with a click on the dais. "Swear it," she demanded.

Tabitha nodded. "Well, of course I'll help find her. I'm sure when Brinley finds out that her mother is still alive, she'll want to help me look." Her face went blank, staring at nothing. "I wonder if she already knows," she mumbled.

Tolarin struck her spear on the dais again. "Swear it," she said.

"Oh," Tabitha said, shaking her thoughts away. "Yes. I swear it."

The three queens regarded her silently a moment, then Halis motioned for Archibald to join them on the dais. Following her instruction, Tabitha took Archibald's hand in her own. "Go now," Halis said, "with the blessing of Nymia and the three queens."

Tabitha curtsied awkwardly, still holding onto Archibald's hand, and the underwater world unraveled around them, twisting into colorful swirls like wet fireworks. She felt Archibald beside her, forced upward by the same invisible current that pushed her, tumbling, toward the sky.

The lake spat them out ungraciously onto the shore. Tabitha felt smooth stones under her hands again and wondered if the whole thing might have been a dream. "Was it all a lie?" she asked, pushing her wet body off the stones, pulling her knees into her chest protectively. "Everything you said to Halis earlier?"

"No," Archibald said. "It was the truth. I did not know that you followed me, or that they would test you. Believe me," he said, dumping water out of his hat with a sigh, "I was just as surprised as you when that snake grabbed me."

"Did you know that she is alive? Brinley's mother, I mean?"

Archibald's voice grew quiet. "No," he said. "Not until they took me." He turned to her. "Do you know where she is? Do you know what has happened to my wife?"

"Not exactly," Tabitha said honestly. "It's true, then, what she said? You really are Brinley's father?"

Archibald stared into his hat thoughtfully. "Yes," he said. "I don't know how to tell her."

She placed a hand on his arm. "You will."

"She already has a father," he said. There was something in his voice that was halfway between bitterness and regret. "I have heard her speak of him. I do not think she would want another."

"That's it!" Tabitha said. "Her father! Archibald, you can help her."

He frowned. "What are you talking about?"

"Her father is lost," Tabitha explained. "He tried to follow her into Aberdeen and he got lost somehow." She shook her head. "We don't understand it, but I know she thinks about it all the time. Maybe you could help her find her father and then . . ." She trailed off, frowning. A moment earlier she had been certain that this would help Archibald's situation but now she couldn't remember how.

"Hmm," Archibald muttered. "Yes. I think I see what you mean. I will speak to Brinley."

Tabitha felt a jolt of panic. "Oh," she said. "Wait, maybe you shouldn't. I don't know if I should have told you that. I think it was a secret."

Archibald chuckled. "Don't worry," he said. "I'm sure she won't mind, so long as I can help."

"You will be able to help," Tabitha said.

He nodded as he got to his feet. The first rays of sunshine were beginning to color the sky. "You were given a great gift tonight," he said, nodding towards the lake.

She shook her head. "I didn't want it. I don't know what to do with it." She felt her heart tighten with fear and questions. "I don't know who I am anymore. I don't know how to be enough for everyone . . ." She stopped as she caught sight of a pair of eyes watching her from the water. Fitz's eyes, she thought, but then they were gone.

Archibald picked her up, set her on her feet. "You are the apprentice to the Mage of Earth, and you are the Magemother's Herald." He looked at her seriously. "And I wouldn't want anyone else protecting my daughter. Most important of all, you are you. And that will always be enough."

THE END